T5-AQQ-294

OTHER YEARLING BOOKS YOU WILL ENJOY:

YEARLING BOOKS are designed especially to entertain and
enlighten young people. Charles F. Reasoner, Professor Emer-
itus of Children's Literature and Reading, New York Univer-
sity, is consultant to this series.

For a complete listing of all Yearling titles, write to
Dell Publishing Co., Inc., Promotion Department,
P.O. Box 3000, Pine Brook, N.J. 07058.

Getting Children Started with Books

On more than one occasion you've probably found yourself having to choose a book for a young child. As you faced an entire rack or shelf of children's books and wondered which one to select, you probably asked yourself: Which book will be appealing? Is it the appropriate reading level?

The book that you have in your hand right now is suited to children who are ages six to nine. Yearling books can be read aloud to children or they can be read independently by those children who are reading on their own.

After a child has read this book alone or with an adult, that child is ready for the suggested activities which follow. These activities follow directly from the story and provide the child with opportunities to think, to explore, and to have fun.

FUN TO READ

FUN TO DO!

After you've read
CAM JANSEN AND THE MYSTERY OF THE U.F.O.
here are some activities you might want to try:

1. Eric takes a pretty amazing photograph with his camera, which wins him an award in the Junior News Photography Contest. If you have a camera, take some pictures. When the pictures are printed, look at them carefully. How could they be improved?

   If you don't have a camera, look at photographs in magazines. What makes an award-winning picture?

2. Visit the library and find a book about U.F.O.s. Learn something new about Unidentified Flying Objects, then teach a friend what you've learned. Discuss whether you think U.F.O.s really exist.

3. Make some drawings of creatures from outer space—what do *you* think such a creature would look like?

4. Can you answer Cam's question: "How would a creature from outer space learn English?"

CAM JANSEN

and
the Mystery of
the U.F.O.

DAVID A. ADLER
Illustrated by Susanna Natti

A Yearling Book

Published by
Dell Publishing Co., Inc.
1 Dag Hammarskjold Plaza
New York, New York 10017

ISBN: 0-440-41142-4

Reprinted by arrangement with The Viking Press
Printed in the United States of America

November 1982

10 9 8 7 6 5 4

CW

For my brother Eddie.
He always made us proud.

Chapter One

One cold November afternoon Cam Jansen and her friend Eric Shelton were walking through town. Eric wanted to enter a photography contest. Cam was helping him look for something to photograph.

Cam picked up a crumpled potato chip bag from the street and held it over a litter basket.

"Take my picture," she said. "You can call it 'Local Girl Cleans Up.'"

"I can't take a posed picture," Eric told her. "You know the rules."

Eric reached into his pocket and took out a page torn from a newspaper.

"Here it is," Eric said, pointing to the page, "rule three."

"I know the rules," Cam said.

Cam closed her eyes and said, "*Click*." She always said, "*Click*," when she wanted to remember something. "My mind is a mental camera," Cam often explained, "and cameras go *click*.

"Announcing our first Junior News Photography Contest," Cam said. Her eyes were still closed. "Grand prize one hundred dollars. Entry rules. One. Only twelve-year-olds and under may enter."

As Cam talked, Eric looked at the contest announcement in the newspaper.

"Two. Photographs must be black-and-white. Three. Photographs must be of local interest. They must not be posed. Four. All entries must be received no later than November thirtieth."

"You did it!" Eric said. "You got every word right!"

People said Cam had a photographic memory. They meant Cam could remember an entire scene. When Cam wanted to remember something, even a detail such as how many buttons were on someone's coat, she just looked at the photograph stored in her brain.

Cam's real name is Jennifer. But people started calling her "The Camera" because of her photographic memory and because she said, "*Click*," so often. Soon "The Camera" was shortened to "Cam."

"Now check me," Cam said. Her eyes were still closed. "I'm going to say the rules backwards.

"Thirtieth—November—than—later—no—received—be—must—entries—all—four—posed—be . . ."

"Enough! Enough!" Eric said. "You're going too fast. I can't keep up."

Cam opened her eyes.

"How did you do that?" Eric asked.

"I have a picture of the rules in my mind. I just read from it."

Cam put her books and lunch box down. "It's cold," she said.

Cam closed the top button of her coat. She pulled down the knitted cap she was wearing until it covered the tops of her ears.

"And it's getting dark," Eric said. "I'm not going to find anything to photograph now. Let's go home."

Eric put the camera back in its case. "I'm never around when anything happens," he complained. "And I'll bet if I am around, either I won't have my camera or I'll be out of film."

"Or," Cam said, "you'll forget to take the lens cap off."

Cam and Eric often spent time together. They were in the same fifth-grade class and lived next door to each other.

"If it wasn't for your hair," Cam's mother often teased, "I'd think you and Eric were twins."

Cam had what people called bright red hair, even though it was more orange than red. Eric's hair was dark brown.

Cam and Eric started walking home. They walked past a row of small stores at the edge of a shopping mall. Then they stopped at the corner and waited for the traffic light to change.

Meow.

Cam and Eric looked up. A gray-and-white kitten was high in a tree. The branch she was standing on was shaking. The kitten took a step toward the end of the branch. The branch shook even more.

Meow.

"I think she wants to come down," Eric said, "but she doesn't know how."

Cam opened her lunch box. "I have part

of a tuna sandwich in here. Maybe I can get the kitten to come down."

Cam reached up and put a piece of tuna fish on the part of the branch closest to the trunk. The kitten saw the food and turned around carefully. The branch shook, but the kitten didn't fall. She walked down the branch and ate the tuna fish. Cam reached out for the kitten.

Eric was holding his camera. "Smile," he said, and he took a picture just as the kitten jumped into Cam's arms.

"I'll call the picture 'Local Girl Saves Untamed Feline.'"

Cam turned to put the kitten down. Then she stopped. She heard noises. Across the street people were shouting and pointing. Cam looked to see what they were pointing at.

In the distance Cam and Eric saw floating green, yellow, blue, and red lights. The lights seemed to brush against one of the trees at the edge of the park. Cam looked straight at the lights and said, "*Click*."

Chapter Two

Eric aimed his camera at the lights. He pressed the shutter button, and the camera went *click*.

The lights were rising, but they weren't going straight up. They were moving from side to side and up and down. It almost seemed that the wind was moving the lights.

Eric aimed his camera again. He pressed the shutter button. *Click.* He pressed it once more. *Click.*

"I'm not sure I'm doing this right." Eric

said. "It's getting dark, and the lights are so far away. I hope at least one picture comes out."

Cam wasn't really listening. She was watching the lights.

"I've seen lights in the sky before," she said, "but they were from helicopters or airplanes or fireworks. I don't know what these are."

"Let's go over there," Eric said, pointing to the parking lot. "Maybe those people know."

Cam put the kitten down. Cam was picking up her books when she heard the kitten cry. The kitten was up in the tree again.

"That cat doesn't seem to learn," Cam said.

"The last time she was up there, you fed her some tuna fish," Eric said. "The kitten learned that if she climbs a tree, she gets something to eat."

12

Cam opened her lunch box. "Well, all I have this time is bread."

Cam reached up and put the bread on the branch. The kitten turned around carefully. She came down the branch and ate the bread.

"I'm going to hold on to you," Cam said as she put the kitten in her coat pocket. "If I don't, you'll just climb that tree again."

Cam and Eric crossed the street. The people in the brightly lit parking lot were all looking up. Some children were taking photographs. A man and a woman were looking through pairs of binoculars.

"Six lights, no, seven," the man said. "Three green lights, two yellow, one blue, and two red. That's eight. I have to get this right if I'm going to write it down."

The man was wearing a big open shoulder bag. A notebook and a book called *Bird Watcher's Guide* were sticking out.

13

"I've got it!" the man said as he put the binoculars in his bag. "Seven flying lights.

"You said we wouldn't see anything," he told the woman next to him, "but you were wrong. We've seen a red-backed sandpiper, a bufflehead, an old-squaw, and now this."

The woman put her binoculars into a case. "It wasn't a sandpiper," she said. "It was a golden plover. The old-squaw you thought we saw was a pintail. And there are eight lights up there, not seven."

Cam and Eric could hardly see the lights now. They were just tiny dots of color.

"Can I look through those?" Cam asked the woman.

The woman took the binoculars out of the case and handed them to Cam.

Cam could see why the couple had trouble counting the lights. Sometimes one would move one way, while another moved in a different direction. Sometimes one light moved behind the others and could not be seen at all. Cam also saw lines, like thin wires, pointing down from each light.

Cam looked straight at the lights and said, *"Click."*

"Let me see," Eric said.

"Just a minute."

The lights were floating up. Cam looked carefully at just one light, a blue one. At

15

first Cam thought it was round, but it wasn't. It was shaped like an egg with a point at the bottom. Cam looked straight at the light and said, "*Click*." Then the lights floated into a cloud and Cam couldn't see them any more.

"They're gone," Cam told Eric. Then she returned the binoculars to the woman.

"Are there seven lights up there or eight?" the woman asked.

"Ah, I'm not sure. The lights keep moving and disappearing. They're hard to count."

"Well, there are eight," the woman said. "I'm sure."

Eric pulled on Cam's sleeve. "I have one picture left. What should it be?"

Cam was going to tell Eric to photograph the crowd, but Eric yelled, "I've got it! Don't move."

Eric bent down and took a picture of the kitten. She was leaning out of Cam's

pocket and eating from someone's bag of groceries.

Cam pulled away. The kitten fell back into her pocket. Some food was still in the kitten's mouth.

"Well, that's it," Eric said. "I hope nothing else happens. I'm out of film."

"Look! Look!" someone in the crowd yelled. "More lights!"

18

Chapter Three

Cam and Eric turned to look. These lights were not a mystery. A fire department light truck drove up and parked nearby. Several of its large, moving beams of light searched the sky. The mysterious lights were just tiny dots of color. They floated in and out of the clouds.

Then a television news truck drove into the parking lot. A young woman holding a microphone got out of the truck. A man holding a television camera followed her.

The woman walked through the crowd

and asked questions. Then she stood facing the cameraman. She took a deep breath, smiled, and spoke into the microphone.

"This is Stephanie Jackson," she said. "I'm here in the parking lot at the corner of Fillmore and Harrison avenues. Just moments ago these people saw several mysterious lights rise into the night. People here are already calling these lights U.F.O.s—unidentified flying objects."

Cam and Eric moved closer to the reporter to hear what she was saying.

"Many U.F.O.s are later found to be weather balloons, kites, clouds, or even high-flying airplanes. Sometimes they are only pranks meant to fool us.

"Others are never identified. Many people believe that some of the truly unidentified flying objects are aircraft from other planets. Some people even claim to have seen strange creatures get off those flying objects.

"We still don't know what was seen here tonight. We may never know."

Stephanie Jackson turned to a man standing nearby. "Sir, can you tell our viewers what you saw?"

The man took off his hat. With his hand he brushed his hair down. He smiled and spoke into the microphone. "I saw lights," he said in a loud voice.

"Yes, well, maybe this girl can tell us more." The reporter held the microphone in front of Cam. With her free hand the reporter turned Cam to face the camera. "What did you see?" she asked.

Cam closed her eyes. She said, "*Click*."

The people near Cam smiled. A few laughed. *Click* was a strange answer to the reporter's question.

"Well, at first," Cam said, "I thought there was just one U.F.O. But the lights moved apart sometimes, so I think there were a lot of small U.F.O.s flying together.

And at one time they were close to the ground. I know that because as they were going up, they touched one of the trees outside the park."

As Cam was speaking, she noticed that Stephanie Jackson was moving away from her. Then Cam saw why. The kitten was leaning out of Cam's coat and licking the reporter's free hand.

"Thank you very much," the reporter said. She walked away quickly.

"But there's more!" Cam said.

"The lights can no longer be seen," the reporter said into the microphone. "They remain a mystery. We don't know what they are or where they came from. But I'm sure the people here tonight will remember what they saw for a long time to come."

The report was over. Stephanie Jackson put the microphone down. She wiped her hand with some tissues. Then she and the

cameraman went back to the truck.

The crowd started to move apart. Some people went to their cars. Others walked across the parking lot to the shopping area.

Cam pulled Eric to a corner of the parking lot. She closed her eyes and said, "*Click*.

"I can't see it!" Cam said. "Come on, Eric. Let's cross the street."

Cam and Eric waited at the corner for the light to change.

"What can't you see?" Eric asked.

"The tree. When the U.F.O.s went up, they hit a tree. I can't see which one it was."

The light changed. Cam and Eric crossed the street.

"The reporter said that some people have seen U.F.O.s land," Cam told Eric. "Creatures from outer space got out. Well, these U.F.O.s hit a tree. They might have landed near the tree."

Cam stood at the corner. She faced the park. "This is where I first saw the U.F.O.s," Cam said. "Sometimes, if I stand where I first saw something, it helps me remember."

Cam closed her eyes. She said, "*Click*."

Then she said, "I see it! It's a small tree between two evergreens. Come on, Eric. Let's go there and take a look. Maybe the U.F.O.s left something behind."

"Something," Eric said, "or someone."

Chapter Four

Cam and Eric were a long way from the park. It was past five o'clock and already quite dark.

"Let's go," Eric said. "It's late. My parents are going out. I have to baby-sit for Howie and the twins tonight. And besides," Eric went on, "we have homework to do. We can come back tomorrow when it's light out."

"Don't worry." Cam told him. "As soon as we've seen what's on the other side of that tree, we'll go home."

Cam felt something moving in her coat pocket. The flap opened and the kitten looked out. Cam petted the back of the kitten's neck. The kitten purred. The flap closed as she settled back into the warmth of Cam's pocket.

"I think you've got yourself a pet," Eric said. "Let's give her a name."

"She likes to climb trees," Cam said as they walked along. "We could call her Twigs or Leaves." Cam thought for a minute. "Or we could give her an outer-space name. After all, we found her and saw a U.F.O. at the same time."

"Well," Eric said, "we can call her Rocket or Stars or Saturn."

"Saturn, that's good," said Cam. "We'll name her after one of the planets. Let's see. There's Mars and Pluto and Neptune. That's a good name for a cat. We'll call her Neptune."

Cam and Eric were getting close to the

park. Cam stopped and looked at the trees.

There were many different evergreens. Evergreens are green all year and are easy to tell apart. But the other trees, the ones without leaves, all looked the same.

Cam closed her eyes. She said, "*Click.* The tree the U.F.O.s hit has white bark. It's a birch between two tall pines."

Cam opened her eyes. "That's the one," she said, pointing.

Cam and Eric walked past the birch tree. The park was empty and dark. The only light came from street lamps outside.

Cam and Eric looked for some hint of a U.F.O. landing. There was nothing near the tree. Toward the center of the park Eric found two ripped balloons.

"Here's something," Cam said. She held up the wrappings from several small pocket flashlights, and a used roll of tape. "But these aren't from outer space."

Cam and Eric kept looking. The ground was covered with leaves. They found cigarette butts, crushed soda cans, and candy-bar wrappers.

Then Cam and Eric heard noises. It sounded like people talking, but they couldn't make out the words. A motor started and bright lights went on. The lights were behind the wall of the handball court.

"Let's see what's over there," Cam whispered.

"No. Let's go back. We have homework."

"We can do it later. Come on."

Cam walked carefully through the leaves. She tried not to make any noise. Eric followed her.

"Look!" Eric said.

A strange-looking creature with wrinkled silver skin ran out. It had a head, arms, and legs and was about the same height as Cam and Eric. Its hands were green and its

feet were blue. It was holding something long and thin.

Then a second creature ran out. It was carrying a pile of colored objects. Both creatures dropped what they were holding and ran back behind the wall.

Chapter Five

Cam and Eric stood still. They were afraid to move.

"What do we do now?" Eric whispered.

"I don't know. Let's just wait."

Cam and Eric waited quietly. They saw one of the creatures run out again. It was holding something.

"Get back here, Cindy," a voice called out. The silver creature dropped what it was holding and ran back behind the wall.

"Did you hear that!" Cam said. "They speak English. Now how would a creature from outer space learn English?"

"Well, maybe they studied it in school," Eric said. "Or maybe they've been here before." Eric thought for a minute. "Or maybe they're wondering how come we speak *their* language."

"Or maybe they're not from outer space," Cam said. "Come on. Let's get closer."

Eric didn't want to get closer. He wanted to go home. But before he could tell Cam, she ran ahead.

She ran from one tree to the next. Eric followed her. They tried to run quietly, but the dried leaves made noise when Cam and Eric stepped on them. Neptune made noise, too. She meowed inside Cam's pocket.

Cam and Eric stopped running when they reached a large tree close to the wall of the handball court. There was a pile of leaves next to the tree. Cam put her lunch box and books down. She tried to hide behind the leaves. She couldn't. The pile was too small.

"Help me," she whispered to Eric. "Let's build this up."

Eric passed leaves to Cam and she placed them on top of the pile. When the pile was high enough, Cam and Eric crawled behind it.

They waited. They watched the wall, but nothing happened. It was quiet.

Cam took Neptune out of her pocket. She stroked the back of her neck. Neptune purred softly.

"If we could see what they dropped behind that wall," Cam said, "we might be able to find out who they are."

Cam put Neptune back in her pocket. Cam crawled around the tree. She got closer to the wall. Then Cam stopped. She heard voices on the other side of the wall.

"Cindy," a boy's voice said, "fold your arms like this. And, Steven, you stand like this."

There was a flash of light on the other side of the wall.

"Steven, you hold the ray gun. Cindy, you sit down next to Steven."

"Oh, Bobby, why can't *I* hold the ray gun?"

Cam crawled closer. She could see a pile of colored objects ahead, behind the wall.

"Don't smile," Cam heard Bobby say. "Look curious."

There was another flash of light.

Cam crawled closer to the wall. The pile of colored objects were children's sneakers, two jackets, an empty box of aluminum foil, and the wrappings from two pairs of green rubber gloves.

Sneakers? Cam thought. *Aluminum foil and rubber gloves?*

Cam sat there. She looked at the sneakers and the coats. *These aren't creatures*

from outer space, Cam told herself. *They're children covered with aluminum foil.*

Cam reached into her pocket. Neptune was still there. She licked Cam's hand and purred.

Then Cam looked back at Eric. He was signaling for Cam to come back. She didn't. She crawled along the back of the wall. There was a large tree just at the edge of the wall. Cam hid behind it and looked out.

A car was parked facing the handball court. Its headlights were on. There were two children covered with aluminum foil. They were both wearing blue wool socks and green rubber gloves. One was holding a toy ray gun. The children's faces were hidden behind silver masks with holes for their eyes and mouths. An older boy, the one called Bobby, was there, too. He was about eighteen. He had a camera and was taking pictures.

It was hard for Cam to see the children and the older boy clearly. The lights from the car reflected off the aluminum foil. Cam held her hand over her eyes to shield them. She looked straight at the two children and said, "*Click*."

Cam heard a noise behind her. Then she felt something poke her in the back.

Cam was afraid to move.

Chapter Six

Without turning around, Cam reached behind her. Something thin and pointed poked her hand. Slowly Cam turned around. It was Eric. He had moved closer to the wall. He was hiding behind a big tree and was trying to get Cam's attention by poking her with a branch.

Cam crawled back to join him. The tree was almost wide enough to hide them both. When Cam looked out, she could clearly see the front of the handball court.

"You were right," Eric said. "They're not from outer space."

Cam and Eric watched while Bobby took photographs. "Bend down," Bobby told Cindy, "like you're looking at something."

"I can't bend. This foil is too tight. Let Steven bend."

Steven crouched down and picked up a leaf. The foil covering his knees ripped. His pants showed through.

"See," Cindy said. "I told you!"

"All right," Bobby said, "hold this newspaper. Hold it like you don't know what it is."

Cindy held the newspaper upside down. Steven put a page into his mouth as if he were trying to eat it.

"Good, very good," Bobby said as he took another picture.

"You know what," Eric whispered to Cam. "I'll bet he's planning to enter the photography contest and win the hundred dollars."

Bobby continued to take photographs.

"No one will believe him," Eric went on. "No one will believe that creatures from outer space landed."

"We almost believed it," Cam said. "After we saw those U.F.O.s take off, we were ready to believe it."

Cam sat behind the tree with her legs crossed and thought. While she sat there,

Neptune crawled out of Cam's pocket and into her lap.

"But how could they have known," Cam asked, "that we would see a U.F.O. tonight?" Cam thought for a minute. "Unless," she said, "the U.F.O.s were a prank and they're the ones who did it."

Eric looked at the handball court.

"They're taking off their masks. What do we do now?"

Cam jumped up. Neptune fell off her lap and ran away.

"Quick!" Cam said. "Take their pictures while they have their costumes half on and half off. A picture like that would prove they're fakes."

Eric held his camera up and looked through it. He pressed the shutter. Nothing happened. Eric pressed it again. Again nothing.

Eric looked at the back of the camera. "Oh, no!" he said. "I'm out of film. I took

the last picture in the parking lot."

Eric opened his camera. He took out the roll of film and put it in his pocket.

"Let's go back," Eric said, "and get someone to help."

Just as Cam and Eric were leaving, they heard Neptune.

Meow.

Neptune was standing on a branch that hung right over the handball court. The branch was shaking.

"Neptune's going to fall," Eric said, "and right on top of Bobby!"

Chapter Seven

Meow.

Neptune raised her right paw. The branch shook.

Neptune fell. She fell right onto Bobby's shoulder. Then Neptune jumped into a pile of aluminum foil. She grabbed a silver mask in her mouth and ran off.

"Get that cat!" Bobby yelled. "Get that mask!"

Bobby dropped his camera and ran after Neptune. Steven and Cindy followed. They chased Neptune around the car, over low bushes, and between trees. They couldn't keep up with Neptune.

But Neptune wasn't running away. She was playing a game. When she saw the others were far behind, she turned around and ran toward them. She ran close and then darted away.

Then Neptune ran to Cam and Eric.

"Quick, let's hide," Eric said. He dived into a pile of leaves.

"No!" Cam yelled. "Let's run."

Cam started to run. She didn't get far. Steven and Cindy caught her. Bobby reached into the pile of leaves and pulled Eric out.

"Look what I found," Bobby said, "a walking tree."

Eric shook the leaves off.

Neptune stopped running. She sat next to Cam and purred. Steven took the mask out of Neptune's mouth.

"What are you doing here?" Bobby asked.

"Watching you," Cam said. "We know Steven and Cindy aren't from another planet."

"No one will believe you took photographs of creatures from another world," Eric said. "And anyway, you can't enter the contest because you're too old."

Bobby laughed.

"I'm entering for him," Cindy said.

"And I'm not worried," Bobby said. "They'll believe me. If they believed that some balloons and flashlights could be a U.F.O., they'll believe creatures from outer space got off and looked around."

"Well," Eric said, "we saw you. We'll tell about what you did."

Bobby laughed again. "Oh, no, you won't. If you don't tell anyone what you saw, we'll share the prize money with you."

"We don't need a share," Cam said. "We'll win the whole hundred dollars by ourselves."

Eric looked at Cam. He didn't know what she was talking about.

"We have pictures of Steven and Cindy with their costumes half off," Cam said. "That proves this whole thing is a fake."

"Give me that!" Bobby said. He grabbed Eric's camera.

While Bobby was opening the camera, Cam reached into Eric's pocket. She took the film out and put it in Neptune's mouth. "Run!" she yelled.

Neptune ran off.

"The cat's got the film," Steven said.

"Get it!" Bobby told Steven and Cindy. "I'll follow in the car."

Steven and Cindy ran after Neptune. Bobby got into the car. He left his camera and camera bag behind. He backed up the car.

Crunch.

The car ran over the camera. Then it went forward and out of the park.

Cam ran over to the broken camera.

"Look," she said. "Their film is ruined. Now they can't enter the contest."

Cam gathered her books and lunch box. Eric closed his camera, put it back into the case, and picked up his books. They walked out of the park.

"I'm glad they can't enter the contest," Eric said. "But it's too bad we lost Neptune."

"Maybe not," Cam said. "There's one place we can look, and it's on the way home.

"I should have known," Cam said as they walked. "The lights were shaped like balloons. Bobby must have taped tiny flashlights to them. That's what made them look like colored lights."

"But how could he be sure the balloons would go up?" Eric asked.

"They were probably filled with helium, like the balloons they sell in the zoo.

"It was dark," Cam went on. "No one was near the park so no one knew what the lights were."

Cam led Eric back to the tree where they first found Neptune.

Meow.

There was Neptune, resting on one of the branches. On the ground right under the branch was Eric's roll of film. He picked it up.

When Neptune saw Cam and Eric, she moved toward the end of the branch. The branch began to shake.

Meow.

Cam held out her arms. "You're not getting any food," she said, "so you might as well come down."

Neptune jumped into Cam's arms, looked up at her, and purred. Cam put Neptune in her coat pocket, picked up her books and lunch box, and started to walk home with Eric.

Cam smiled. "Now," she said to Eric, "we can go home and do our homework."

Chapter Eight

There weeks later Cam was at Eric's house. They were watching the evening news on television. Cam was sitting on the floor holding Neptune. Eric was sitting on the couch. His baby brother, Howie, was in his arms drinking from a bottle.

"And now," the television reporter said, "let's go to Stephanie Jackson, who is standing by."

Stephanie Jackson's picture came on the television screen. "The winners in the Junior News Photography Contest have just been announced," she said.

"This is it!" Cam said.

Stephanie Jackson held up a photograph of a window washer. He was cleaning the windows of one of the city's tallest buildings. A bird had landed on his head.

"This is the winning photograph. It was taken by eleven-year-old Karen Grey."

Stephanie Jackson held up two other photographs. The first was of a crowd of people watching the U.F.O.s.

The second photograph was of Neptune. Neptune was leaning out of Cam's pocket and was eating from someone's bag of groceries.

"These two photographs were awarded honorable mention. One was taken by twelve-year-old Michael Wagner. The other was taken by ten-year-old Eric Shelton. Congratulations."

"I won! I won!" Eric shouted.

Cam smiled. "We always talk about my amazing mental camera," she said, "but I think you and your camera are pretty amazing, too."